Hungry Giant's Shoe

HAMERAY
PUBLISHING GROUP

The Hungry Giant was in a bad mood.

He hopped on one foot and yelled,

"I can't find my new red shoe.

Little people! Find my shoe for me!"

"Yes, yes, Hungry Giant,"
the people replied,
and they ran into the giant's house.

They looked and looked for the shoe.

No. It was not in the giant's house.

"Find my new red shoe!"
roared the giant.

The people put their hands
over their ears
and ran back to town.

The giant's roar came after them.
"Find my shoe! Find my shoe!"

"Yes, Hungry Giant!" they cried.
"We will find your shoe!"

What a lot of fuss!

What a lot of running!

The people looked in every street.

They looked in every shop.

They looked in every house.

But they did not find the giant's shoe.

The people said, "Oh brother!
We told the giant we'd find his shoe!
What will we do?"

Some children came down the river
in a beautiful boat.

"What are you looking for?" they said.

The people replied, "The Hungry Giant
has lost his new red shoe."

The children looked at their boat.
It was big and red and new.
"Oh-oh!" the children said.

The people took the shoe
to the Hungry Giant.
"Here it is!" they said.

The giant was very happy.
"My shoe!" he cried.
"My lovely new red shoe!"

But soon the giant's bad mood
came back.

He roared and roared.

"I've got a wet foot!"